Tales of
Holidays

Also by Pleasant DeSpain

THE BOOKS OF NINE LIVES

VOLUME FIVE

Tales of Holidays

Pleasant DeSpain

Illustrations by Don Bell

August House Publishers, Inc.
LITTLE ROCK

Published 2002 by August House Publishers, Inc.
P.O. Box 3223, Little Rock, Arkansas, 72203,
501-372-5450.

Printed in the United States of America

10 9 8 7 6 5 4 3 2 1 HB

LIBRARY OF CONGRESS CATALOGING-IN-PUBLICATION DATA
DeSpain, Pleasant.
  Tales of holidays / by Pleasant DeSpain ; [Don Bell, illustrator].
  p. cm. — (Books of nine lives ; v. 5)
  Contents: Twelve months (Czechoslovakia)—Babushka (Russia)—The little
juggler (France)—Christina's Christmas cookies (Scandinavia)—The baker's
dozen (United States)—The Hanukkah bowl (Russia)—St. Valentine
(Italy)—Whooooo (United States)—The lost fiddler (Wales).
  ISBN 0-87483-667-0
  1. Holidays—Folklore. 2. Tales. [1. Holidays—Folklore. 2. Folklore] I. Bell,
Don, 1935– ill. II. Title
  PZ8.1.D453 Taj 2002
  398.23'6—dc21   2002025569

Executive editor: Liz Parkhurst
Text designer: Joy Freeman
Cover and book illustration: Don Bell

AUGUST HOUSE   PUBLISHERS   LITTLE ROCK

For Bob and JoAnn DeSpain,
my brother and sister-in-law,
with love and appreciation.

Acknowledgments

I'm fortunate to have genuine friends and colleagues without whose help the continuation of this series would not have been possible. Profound thanks to:

- Liz and Ted Parkhurst, Publishers
- Don Bell, Illustrator
- Joy Freeman, Project Editor
- Margaret Read MacDonald, Storyteller, Author, Librarian
- Jennifer D. Murphy, Head of the Children's Department, Albany, New York, Public Library
- Candace E. Deisley, Youth Services Librarian Albany, New York, Public Library
- Denver Public Library
- Lakewood, Colorado, Public Library
- Seattle Public Library
- University of Washington Library (Seattle)

The Books of Nine Lives Series

A good story lives each time it's read and told again. The stories in this series have had many lives over the centuries. My retellings have had several lives in the past twenty-plus years, and I'm pleased to witness their new look and feel. Two or three of the tales found in each of volumes 4 and 5 include previously published works (indicated by asterisks). They were originally published in "Pleasant Journeys," my weekly column in *The Seattle Times*, during 1977-78 and collected into a two-volume set entitled *Pleasant Journeys: Tales to Tell from Around the World*, in 1979. The books were republished as *Twenty-Two Splendid Tales to Tell from Around the World* a few years later and remained in print for twenty-one years and three editions.

Now, in 2002, this series of thematically based, multicultural collections continues.

These timeless, ageless, universal, useful, and so very-human tales deserve to be read and told again.

I'm profoundly grateful to all the teachers, parents, storytellers, and children who have found these tales worthy of sharing. One story always leads to the next. As evolving human beings, we are more alike than we are different, each with a story to tell.

—*Pleasant DeSpain*
Troy, New York

Holiday Notes

New Year's Day: January 1

People throughout the world celebrate the end of the old year and the arrival of the new one. January was named for the Roman god Janus. He was the god with two faces, one looking back and one looking forward. Today, an old man often represents year's end, just as a newborn child represents the year ahead. New Year's is the time of fresh starts. Debts are paid, arguments forgiven, and New Year's resolutions set. Ultimately, New Year's represents change from the old and growth with the new.

Christmas: December 25

The major Christian holiday celebrates the birth of Jesus. The Bible explains that Jesus, the Son of God, was born to a woman named Mary. The night before His birth, a bright star appeared in the sky shining down upon a stable. It guided three kings from afar to the holy place. They carried gifts for the Child. The custom of gift giving continues, but it wasn't until the nineteenth century that Saint Nicholas became the popular figure called Santa Claus.

Hanukkah: December

The Jewish holiday of Hanukkah is known as the Festival of Lights. Eight menorah candles are lit to commemorate miracles. After a successful battle led by Judah Maccabee more than twenty-one hundred years ago, a small Jewish army discovered that the Eternal Light, a lamp in the Holy Temple in Jerusalem, had gone out. They found a small vial of oil for the lamp, enough to burn for one day. Yet the oil burned for eight days. This is why Hanukkah is observed for eight days. It's customary to eat potato latkes during this sacred time because they are made with oil.

St. Valentine's Day: February 14

This special holiday began in ancient Rome with a festival called Lupercalia. Dedicated to lovers, it was celebrated in mid-February. The custom of the day was for maidens to place their names in a decorated box. The young men drew from the box the name of the girl who would be his partner for the coming year. The popular symbol of this holiday is Cupid, the Roman god of love. The gift of red roses was also a Roman symbol of love. It was believed as well that wild birds chose their mates on February 14.

Halloween: October 31

In ancient times, the Celts lived in England, Ireland, and northern France. They held a festival to mark the end of harvest season and the beginning of winter. They called it Samhain (pronounced *Sah-ween*). The Celts believed that witches and ghosts and the souls of the dead roamed free on this one night. In the ninth century, the Catholic Church named November 1 as All Saints' Day, or All Hallows. Thus the night before was called All Hallows Eve—or Halloween. Some of the old pagan beliefs and customs regarding ghosts and spirits continue as part of today's celebrations.

Contents

Introduction

The word *holiday*, derived from "holy day," is defined as a day of festivity or recreation on which no work is done. Stories about and for holidays usually result from human experiences deemed special, holy, or even supernatural, as in the case of Halloween or Passover.

Like most people, I love holidays. Not only do they provide a time for rest but, more importantly, for celebration of the human spirit.

I often share a true story of love and goodwill during the Christmas season. During the 1980s, a junior high school lad living in Buena Vista, Colorado, came to school dressed in an old sweatshirt to keep out the December mountain cold. The kind-hearted teachers took up a collection and presented him with a fleece-lined denim jacket. He thanked them and wore it home. It snowed that night, and the following morning he arrived at school again wearing just his sweatshirt. When asked the where-abouts of the coat, the boy explained that he had wrapped it up as a gift for his mother. She had no coat to wear. The teachers bought him another jacket and told him that he couldn't give this one away. Truly, it is blessed to give as well as receive.

The stories in this collection contain spirit. They are multicultural and festive. Their origins include Czechoslovakia, France, Russia, Scandinavia, Wales, Italy, and the United States. I've told them in schools, at celebrations, and at holiday parties, again and again, during the past thirty years. They don't grow old. They do grow better. It's all in the sharing. Tell them well.

Twelve Months

Czechoslovakia

There once was a beautiful young girl named Natalia whose life was hard. Her mother died and her father remarried a cruel woman, now her stepmother. One day her father left the cottage and didn't return. Even worse, Marishka, the stepmother's mean-spirited daughter, blamed Natalia for her father's disappearance. Both mother and daughter made the poor girl's life miserable.

"Natalia, chop more wood for the fire and be quick about it," Marishka cried.

"Sweep the floor, cook the dinner, wash

the dishes," ordered the stepmother. "Don't even think about going to bed tonight, Natalia. I want you to sew a new dress for me."

Natalia did as she was told and never complained. This was her life, and she decided to make the best of it. The years went by, and Natalia grew even more beautiful. This outraged her stepmother and stepsister.

One frozen morning in late December, Natalia's stepmother said, "I miss the sweet smell of violets in the house. Go into the forest, daughter. Pluck an armful of violets and bring them to me. If you fail to do this, you may not return home."

"But stepmother, it's winter. Violets do not bloom in the snow."

"Don't argue with me. Bring me violets or suffer the consequences."

Natalia put on her tattered coat and torn

scarf and walked deep into the white forest. Snow-clad trees stood tall and silent as she passed by. Suddenly she spied smoke rising from a glen. She approached cautiously. Twelve strange men sat around the bright fire. All wore long woolen hooded robes. Some were old, and some were young. Some looked tired, while others looked fresh. They made no sound. All Natalia heard was the crackling of the burning logs.

The oldest of the twelve sat on a golden throne at the top of the circle. The other eleven sat on silver chairs with high backs. It was the oldest who saw Natalia shivering in the trees.

"Step out from your hiding place, maiden," he called. "Why have you come to our secret grove?"

"I seek violets for my stepmother, kind sirs."

"Violets do not grow in the snow," he

responded in a tired voice. "Surely you know that."

"I do, good sir, but my stepmother insists. I may not return home until I find an armful."

The twelve men held a brief conversation around the fire. Natalia heard a few of the words spoken aloud—words such as *December, winter snows, March, violets*, and *months yet*. A decision was made. The old man got up slowly from his throne and stood behind it. A young man moved from his silver chair and sat on the chair of gold.

"I'm March," he explained. "The man behind me is Old December. We are the twelve months of the year. You'll witness a miracle, but only for a short while. Gather the flowers while you can."

Dark clouds gave way to the golden sun, and gray skies turned blue. Snow melted, and icy streams ran free. Grass sprouted tall and green, and bright blue violets sprang up from the forest floor. Natalia's mouth fell open in wonder.

"Quickly," shouted March. "Take the flowers. I can only remain in Old December's seat for another minute."

Natalia plucked an armful, thanked the twelve months for their kindness, and ran home. A snowfall, heavy and wet, followed her every step.

Bursting through the cottage door, she startled her stepmother. "Here are the violets you asked for," she said. "Shall I put them in a vase?"

"Where? Where did you find these? Tell me at once."

"In a grove of tall trees, deep in the forest. The flowers were under the snow."

Natalia's stepmother and stepsister whispered together long into the night. The next morning it was Marishka who said, "I want strawberries for my cereal, Natalia. Fetch me a basket of ripe strawberries."

"Strawberries are a summer fruit," complained Natalia. "Where will I find ripe strawberries?"

"The same place you found the violets," said her stepmother. "And you may not return home without them."

Natalia put on her thin winter coat and torn scarf. She trudged though the deep snow, back to the sacred glen. The twelve months sat around the blazing fire as before, with Old December gracing the golden throne.

"Young maiden, you have returned," said the old man. "What do you seek on this cold morning?"

"Ripe strawberries, kind sir. My stepmother says I can't go home without them."

"Very well," sighed the old man. "June, be good enough to take my seat."

The moment Young June sat on the golden chair, a hot wind blew through the forest. Snow vanished from the tree limbs, and squirrels ran out to play. Bushes with red, ripe strawberries, plump and sweet, covered the ground.

"Hurry, maiden, gather as many as you can. I can't sit here long, as it isn't my time."

Natalia's hands became a blur as she grabbed, picked, and plucked. Her basket filled, the wind turned to ice and the snow began to fall. Old December had reclaimed his throne.

She ran home to the cottage and placed the basket of strawberries in her stepsister's hands. "I hope this satisfies you, Marishka."

"Where? Where did you gather these?" demanded her stepmother.

"In the same grove of trees where I found the violets."

More whispering between stepmother and

daughter took place. Natalia made out some of the words: *secret grove...strawberries in December...we'll be rich!*

The following morning, Marishka put on her warmest coat, fur hat and boots, and walked into the forest. Following Natalia's frozen footsteps, she soon came to the sacred grove. The twelve months sat round the fire. Old December kept the place of honor.

"Tell us, maiden, what do you seek?"

"What I seek is my business and none of your own," she replied.

Old December frowned and waved his long, cold fingers three times in the air. The fire and all twelve months vanished in a puff of gray smoke. An icy wind descended and snow began to fall. Marishka ran from the grove and was soon lost beyond hope. She failed to return to the cottage that day. Her mother went in search of her the next morning. She, too, lost her way and never made it home.

Natalia stayed on in the cottage and waited for Spring. Three months later, she picked violets in the forest and sang with the birds. Three months after that, she plucked strawberries from the vines and laughed with the summer breeze. It wasn't long before she fell in love with a young nobleman, whom she married. Natalia lived a long and happy life.

Babushka

Russia

Long ago in late December, the Star of Bethlehem shone bright in the night sky. In a country far away, a woman of age named Babushka rocked in her chair. It was a still and cold night. The branches of trees were covered with ice. The wind blew hard for a moment, then stopped, as if listening for the advancing dawn.

"It's a strange night," Babushka whispered to herself, "strange and cold. I'm happy to sit right here, in front of my warm fire."

Suddenly a loud knock came to her

wooden door. Babushka was startled. "Who's there? Who comes on such a night?"

"Travelers," came the reply from the other side of the door. "We mean you no harm, dear lady. We've come to ask you to join us."

"Join you? To go where?" She opened the door. Three noblemen, dressed in fine woolen robes and carrying lavish gifts, stood before her.

"The Christ Child is born in Bethlehem tonight," said the first prince among men.

"We journey to greet Him and offer gifts," said the second.

"You are a good woman, Babushka. Come with us to Bethlehem."

"Tonight isn't for traveling," she answered. It is so very cold. Better to go in the morning with the sun at our backs."

"We cannot wait, Babushka."

"I cannot leave my fire tonight. Thank you for stopping by with your good news."

The wind howled and Babushka closed her door. The three wise men continued on their journey.

The old woman rocked before the blazing fire, remembering the beauty that shines in the eyes of babes. She remembered how it feels to rock a newborn and sing him a

lullaby. Sighing, she said aloud, "Tomorrow. I'll catch up with those nice men tomorrow, and go meet the Child."

At sunrise, Babushka filled a basket with balls of red yarn, wooden toy soldiers, pretty

blue and gold ribbons, and beautifully decorated eggshells. She knew how to delight a
baby. She put on her warmest cloak, boots,
and gloves, and began following in the path
of the travelers. The night wind, however,
had covered their tracks with fresh snow.

Her old eyes missed a turn in the road,
and it wasn't long before she was lost. She
knocked at the door of a stranger's house.
"Excuse me," she said to the man who
answered, "I seek the Christ Child. I bring
him gifts. Can you point the way?"

The man shook his head no and said,
"Farther on...you must travel farther on."

Babushka kept walking, asking everyone
she met on the road if they knew the way to
Bethlehem. "It's farther on, old woman,"
came the replies.

And thus she travels to this very day,
always in search of the Child. Each year on
the Eve of Christmas Day, she comes into

the bedrooms of sleeping children and asks, "Is this the one I seek? Is this Him?" Realizing that it isn't, she takes a gift from her basket and sets it on the child's pillow.

And Babushka continues her travels...farther on...farther on....

The Little Juggler

France

More than seven hundred years ago, a
boy named Barnaby made his way in the
world as a street performer. Walking from village to village, he followed the crowds to the
market place and set to work. His singing
voice was sweet and he was a skilled tum-
bler, but juggling was his true art. Barnaby
kept five red apples in the air without drop-
ping a single piece of fruit. Tossing seven colorful hoops up high, he juggled them round
and round until his audience clapped long
and loud. The boy also had a winning smile.

When it came time to put a coin in his hat, the audience rewarded him handsomely.

Barnaby's mother died when he was a baby. His father taught him how to entertain a crowd, but he was robbed and killed by a highwayman the year before. Barnaby was now an orphan who survived with wit and skill.

The boy loved springtime best, as people were happy to be outside after a long winter. They flocked to the market squares and showered him with coins. Barnaby ate and slept soundly during the spring. Summer was a marvelous season as well. The juggling boy traveled far and wide during the summer months. Many more people gathered to watch his routines and applaud him.

Autumn was a difficult time. Fewer people came to market, and when the wind blew hard, he often dropped his props. But winter was the cruelest season. Markets closed and heavy snows made roads impassable. With little shelter from the icy winds, Barnaby shivered in his thin woolen cloak.

One frozen November morning, a kind monk named Brother Thomas came upon the juggler crouched in a doorway. "Where do you live?" asked the monk.

"Everywhere and nowhere, brother," the boy replied. "The street is my home."

"Then you must come to the abbey. You will have a roof over your head and food in your belly."

Barnaby followed the monk through deep snowdrifts to the abbey. Home to one hundred monks, it was a large and busy place. Barnaby's chores included sweeping long hallways and polishing copper pots and pans. He didn't mind. He was pleased to be able to help those who were helping him.

Christmas drew near. Each monk made a special gift to lay at the feet of a beautiful statue standing gracefully in the corner of the chapel. It was Mother Mary holding the Christ Child in her arms.

"I'm baking a special loaf of herb bread for Our Lady," said the baker.

"I found a piece of gold while digging in the garden. I'm giving it to Our Lady," said the monk who raised roses and grew vegetables.

"I'm writing new words to an old song," explained the choirmaster.

"What will you give, Barnaby?" asked the monk who brought him to the abbey.

"I know not, Brother Thomas. I have nothing worthy of Our Lady."

Barnaby grew sad. After finishing his chores, he went to his small room and prayed. "What can I give you, Mother Mary? What can I make for you and the Child?"

No answers came, and the boy's misery increased.

Long icicles hung down from the abbey's rafters on the frozen night of Christmas Eve. The monks donned thick robes and wrapped their feet in burlap sacks. Still they shivered while chanting and singing. Then they lay all their special offerings at the feet of the divine statue. A solitary tear froze on Barnaby's cheek.

When the final gift, a beautifully illustrated manuscript, was offered, the monks closed their eyes and prayed for a glorious new year. The moment Barnaby closed his eyes, he felt something in his heart. He saw something in his imagination. He knew what to do!

When the last monk left the chapel, the boy raced back to his room and threw off his robe. He put on his tights and colorful cape. He gathered up his hoops and apples, and hurried back to the chapel. After lighting several tall candles, Barnaby stood before Our

Lady with his head bowed. "Sweet Mother," he prayed. "I cannot read nor write on parchment. I do not know how to paint beautiful pictures or make new words to songs. I have neither gold nor bread to offer. I can only give what I have. And what I have is this…"

Barnaby began his tumbling routine, first leaping about the room with handsprings, then turning graceful somersaults. He circled the room twice, then stopped. It was time to juggle. He tossed two apples in the air, then two more, and finally the fifth. Around and around, faster and faster they flew, creating a circular blur of red. He dropped the apples and picked up the seven hoops. Higher and higher they danced, his hands chopping the air, never missing a beat.

He juggled with perfection. He juggled with love. It was his greatest moment, his finest show. He caught all seven hoops with one hand and set them on the smooth stone floor. Barnaby closed his eyes and bowed his head. He had a feeling that his mother and father, watching from heaven above, were proud of their son.

They were not the only ones pleased with the gift. Barnaby looked up to see a smile grace Mary's lips. "You have given the greatest gift of all, Barnaby, the gift of yourself."

The Christ Child cooed in agreement.

Mary and the Child turned to stone once again. Barnaby gathered his props and, leaving the chapel, bumped into Brother Thomas standing at the door.

"I saw all," he said with tears in his eyes. "You are blessed, dear boy. You have a permanent home with us."

Barnaby studied hard and became a brother. And he juggled for Our Lady and the Child, each year on Christmas Eve, for the rest of his life.

Christina's Christmas Garden*

Scandinavia

Young Christina lived with her old mother in the deepest part of the forest. Their home was a cave carved out of the side of a mountain wall. They were so poor that village children called them "Beggar Girl" and "Beggar Mother."

They constructed a crude door of boughs and branches at the cave's entrance to keep out the cold winds. Smooth stones covered the floor. Beggar Mother cooked simple meals in an iron pot that hung over the fire pit. They slept on beds of straw, and for clothing they wore animal skins.

Whenever they saw Christina, the village children chanted:

> *Beggar Girl looks like a bear!*
> *Beggar Girl runs like a hare!*

She'd been scorned by the villagers all her life, but she wasn't bitter or angry. The entire forest knew that Christina was loving and kind.

Whenever her mother returned to the cave from a day of begging, the girl would spread bread crumbs on the ground for birds and squirrels. She knew where to find wild berries and sweet honey. She knew which trees dropped the biggest and best-tasting nuts. She dug for roots and often found the hiding places of wild onions. Christina carried cold spring water to the cave each day and always played gentle games with the wild animals.

Now it was winter, and the frozen forest slept under a heavy blanket of snow.

Christina looked into the windows of the villagers' homes and knew that it was Christmas Eve. Hearty meals were set on tables, and colorfully wrapped gifts were piled high under candlelit Christmas trees. Families gathered around warm fireplaces to sing songs of peace and goodwill, but when they saw Beggar Girl peeking into their fes-tivities, they chased her away with angry words. She belonged to the forest, not to them.

Christina trudged through the snow until she came to the little church on the edge of the village. Old Brother Peter cared for the church. The pews were trimmed with pine boughs for Christmas, and he was ready to ring the big iron bell that hung in the belfry. The rope was frozen stiff, however, and he hadn't the strength in his cold fingers to make it ring.

Christina liked Brother Peter. She often brought him dead branches from the forest to warm his winter fire. In spite of the blinding snow, the small girl quickly climbed up to the belfry and yanked on the frozen rope once, twice, three times! The ice-covered bell began to ring, and crisp, loud notes announced Christmas Eve.

Something wonderful began to happen. As Christina rang the bell, the snow melted and the forest turned green. Flowers of every color sprang up from the earth, and the bees and butterflies danced in the air. Birds, squirrels, rabbits, and chipmunks appeared, and their happy songs and chatterings broke the once-cold silence.

Sweet strawberries and plump blackberries ripened on tangled vines, and in the distance, the bubbling of the brook could be

heard. A warm sun poured light and life into the darkest corners of the forest while white doves circled on quiet wings.

The villagers ran from their houses and watched with wonder as Christina climbed down the belfry's steep steps and began walking home. Flowers bloomed wherever she stepped, and butterflies fluttered happily above her head. Christina laughed, and the villagers, feeling her joy, laughed with her. The entire forest was Christina's Christmas garden.

The next morning, however, the forest was covered with a fresh blanket of snow, for it had to return to its cold winter sleep.

The Baker's Dozen*

United States

Long ago, when the city of Albany, New York, was but a quaint Dutch village, a baker by the name of Van Amsterdam ran a successful business. His bread, cookies, and cakes were delicious, and he sold a big batch each day.

During the Christmas holidays Master Van Amsterdam baked a special cookie in the shape of Saint Nicholas. People came from several nearby communities to purchase them for holiday feasts. The day before Christmas was especially busy. The baker worked hard to keep up with all the orders and was happy when the sun began to set. He could now close his door.

Before he counted the money from the day's sales, an ugly old woman banged on the door and demanded to be let in. Van Amsterdam had a few dozen cookies in the glass case, so he opened the door. She wore a stained and patched cloak along with a tall peaked hat. Her crooked nose was too long for her face. She pointed to the Saint Nicholas cookies and said in a squeaky voice, "I'll take a dozen."

The baker counted out twelve, wrapped them in brown paper, and tied the package with string.

"That's only twelve. I want a dozen. Give me another," she said.

"I gave you a dozen. A dozen means twelve."

"Wrong," she said. "Twelve plus one more

makes a dozen. I want a dozen."

"I'm too tired for such nonsense," replied the baker. "Everyone knows that a dozen means twelve. Take the dozen I've given you and leave me in peace."

As the old woman turned to leave, she said, "You've cheated me out of one cookie. I won't forget it. Nor will you."

The new year began, and everything went wrong in the bakery. One day Van Amsterdam removed a pan of cookies from the oven and placed them on the counter. A customer came in and said that he wanted all of them, but the baker found it impossible to lift them from the pan. Even though he had greased it, the cookies stayed stuck.

On the following day he took another pan of cookies from the oven and watched in horror as each cookie slid to the pan's edge and tumbled to the floor. On the third day all the cookies he baked shrank to one half of their original size.

Soon he had little to sell, and his usual customers went to other bakeries. Master Van Amsterdam prayed to Saint Nicholas himself for advice.

The kindly saint appeared in his dream that night and said, "You are a good baker and have a prosperous business. I suggest that you be more generous to others."

The next morning the old woman was his first customer. "I'd like a dozen of your best cookies."

The baker counted out thirteen and wrapped them up for her. She paid him and began to leave. As she opened the door, she said, "As long as you remain generous, no more trouble will haunt you. From this day forward, a baker's dozen is thirteen."

And so it became a custom in the villages and colonies to give extra measure as a sign of generosity.

The Hanukkah Bowl

Russia

Some folk say that the people of Chelm are fools. Some say that they are wise. Some say they are the wisest fools on earth. You'll have to decide.

The winter was unusually bleak. The people of Chelm were cold and hungry. A stranger came to town during Hanukkah week. He may have been a beggar. He may have been a thief. He carried a canvas bag containing a blue mixing bowl, a hand grater, and a long wooden spoon. The bowl looked ordinary. You could buy one like it from any shopkeeper. But this one was special. It was the Hanukkah Bowl, the most extraordinary bowl the people of Chelm had ever seen.

It was snowing when the stranger arrived. He knocked on several doors, saying, "Please let me in. I'm cold and I'm hungry. I'll perish in this storm."

"Go away. Go away." He heard it again and again. "We have nothing to spare."

"Go to the synagogue," yelled a woman. "You'll find shelter there."

He trudged through the snow and, finding the synagogue's door unlocked, went in. Pavel, the old caretaker, sat before the hot stove in the corner of the main room. Closing the door behind him, the stranger joined the caretaker on the bench. He warmed his hands and feet while thinking things over.

"What brings you to Chelm on a day like this?" asked Pavel.

"It's Hanukkah week," replied the stranger, "and I want to show the good people of Chelm my magic bowl. It makes latkes fit for the rabbi's table."

"A bowl that makes latkes? I've never heard of such a thing. Show me how it's done."

The stranger took the blue bowl from his canvas sack and placed it on the bench. "Of course, if I had just a bit of local flour, the latkes will taste better. I always think that local is best, don't you?"

"Yes, I do," replied the man. "We mill the finest flour in the country, right here in Chelm. I'll get you some."

While fetching the flour, Pavel told several others about the stranger with the blue bowl that could make latkes. A small crowd of townsfolk followed him back to the synagogue and gathered to watch.

The stranger took the grater and spoon

from his bag and set them next to the bowl. "The flour is perfect," he said, "but the bowl needs a pinch of salt and a dash of pepper, to flavor the latkes."

"I'll get them," volunteered the baker's wife. "Is there anything else?"

"I'm sure that Chelm's chickens would like to help," explained the stranger. "Perhaps a few of their largest eggs?"

"Of course our chickens want to help. It's Hanukkah, after all. I'll be right back."

While she was gone, the stranger said, "The bowl doesn't like anything sticking to its sides. I wonder if any of you have a drop or two of oil to spare? And an onion, per-haps? The bowl loves an onion."

Fascinated by the magical bowl, the schoolteacher said, "I'll get the oil, and my wife's onion basket is full. I'll borrow one. She'll never know."

"Now what am I missing?" asked the

stranger. "Something, something…if only I could put my finger on it."

"Potatoes," cried three of the women. "A bowl can't make latkes without potatoes."

"And a carrot," said the shoemaker. "I always like the taste of a grated carrot in my latkes. I'll get the potatoes if you'll add a carrot."

"Indeed I will," said the stranger. "After all, these latkes must be fit for the rabbi."

With all ingredients at hand, the stranger went to work. The townsfolk watched his every move. He peeled, cut, and grated the potatoes and carrot into the bowl. He stirred in the flour with the long wooden spoon. He beat the eggs and grated the onion, and into the bowl they went.

The mayor arrived and asked, "What is going on?"

"The blue bowl is making latkes fit for the rabbi," said several voices at once.

"But we need someone special to add the
final touch, Mayor," explained the stranger.
"Would you be so good as to add the salt and
pepper?"

Pleased to be asked, the mayor sprinkled
with flair.

"The bowl has done its work," said the
stranger. "Now, who has a big skillet and a
hot fire?"

"Me!" cried three of the women.

They went from house to house, cooking
latkes in each. At last, the golden pancakes

were ready for tasting. The citizens of Chelm
followed the stranger right to the rabbi's door.
The rabbi, surprised that a crowd stood on
his porch, asked what was happening.

The stranger offered him a latke and said,
"Please taste this."

The rabbi took a healthy bite, chewed,
and swallowed. He wiped his chin. "Why,
that's the best Hanukkah latke I've ever
eaten!" he said with a big grin. The people
cheered and patted the stranger on the back.

"And all from the blue bowl," said one.

"It's the Hanukkah Bowl," cried another.

"Where can we get a bowl like that?"
asked a third.

"I'll give you mine," said the stranger, "but
only if you'll make a promise. When a cold
and hungry stranger knocks on your doors
during Hanukkah Week, promise that you'll
invite him in."

Everyone promised, and the stranger

presented his blue bowl to the townsfolk.
And every year during this blessed time,
they use it to make latkes fit for the rabbi.
And every stranger who happens by is
invited in. He's warmed and fed, and told the
story of Chelm's Hanukkah Bowl.

St. Valentine

Italy

Valentine's Day was named for a Christian priest who lived in the third century. Christians were persecuted during this early time because they refused to worship the Roman gods. They were often arrested and placed in prison for their beliefs.

Valentine was not afraid. He held worship services in public places and tried to convert as many Romans as possible to Christianity. He lived and worked in constant danger.

One day, the ruler of the Roman Empire,

Emperor Claudius II, made a startling announcement. "I want a thousand men for a new army. They must be young, strong, and willing to fight. And most important, they cannot be married. From this day forth, I forbid the young men of Rome to marry."

"Why?" asked Rome's youth. "Why can't we marry?"

"Because married men are reluctant to leave their wives and children and march off to fight wars in distant lands," came the official reply.

Brother Valentine thought this new decree unfair. He gave sermons on the beauty of love and the joys of marriage. He spoke often about the power of the heart and how love represented the joy of heaven here on earth. Several young couples pleaded with him to marry them in secret. Knowing the risks, he agreed.

Nearly one hundred couples converted to

Christianity and were married by Brother Valentine. Whispers throughout Rome confirmed that the Christian priest was the solution to the marriage ban.

The Emperor was outraged. "Find and arrest this priest. We'll put him on trial."

Brother Valentine was captured and thrown into prison. It wasn't long before couples in love and those he had married arrived at the prison with fresh flowers. They tossed them over the walls and left them on the ground. Often notes were attached: THANK YOU. WE LOVE YOU. BLESS YOU.

The jailer's eldest daughter was blind. It was her job to sweep the walkway outside the prison wall each afternoon. She loved to gather the bouquets of flowers and inhale their sweet fragrances. She spoke often with Valentine and brought him extra food and clean water. The priest told her stories of his travels and adventures in return. He was

jailed for an entire year before the public trial was held.

Valentine, brought before Claudius II in chains, wore his tattered robe with dignity. He stood tall and appeared at ease. The Emperor was impressed.

"Valentine," he ordered, "denounce your false beliefs. Give up your religion, and from this day forth, worship the Roman gods. Do so, and I'll grant your freedom."

The good brother lowered his head and

said a silent prayer. Then he looked into the cold eyes of the Emperor. "I cannot surrender that which fills my heart," he said in a gentle voice. "My faith is my life."

"You give me no choice," said Claudius. He ordered the priest to be put to death.

Valentine was returned to his cell for the night. Throughout the long dark hours, he prayed. He prayed for those he had married and for the jailer's blind daughter. He gathered a handful of flowers strewn about the floor of his cell and bound them with twine. He attached a message for the blind girl: FROM YOUR VALENTINE.

The Christian priest was publicly beheaded on the morning of February 14. On the anniversary of his death we still send fresh flowers and love notes to those we care for. We call them "valentines."

Whooooo

American South

Beware if you venture forth on Halloween night. You might discover the *whooooo*, and that will be the end of you.

It began long ago with seven witches who lived in an evil woods. It was Halloween night, and the crones gathered round a steaming cauldron in a tumble-down shack. Into the boiling vat they tossed the eye of bat, the wing of gnat, and the tail of rat. Into the bubbling brew they offered a pinch of mud, a smidgen of blood, and a red rosebud.

"The night is black," said the first witch.

"The night is cold," spat the second.

"The night is ripe," cackled the third.

"The night is full of fright!" screamed the fourth.

"Tonight we fly," whispered the fifth.

"My oh my!" exclaimed the sixth.

"My oh my..." echoed the seventh.

Knock. Knock. Knock.

"Who's at our broken door?" asked the first witch. "Who could it be on this special night?"

"It's the wind," answered the second witch, "the wind is lonely tonight."

"Go away, Wind," hollered the third. "We have no time."

Louder it came. *Knock. Knock. Knock.* Then a hollow voice: "Let me in...let me in...It's cold out here. Let me innnnn."

"Go away, we say," said the fourth.

"We say, go away!" repeated the fifth.

Louder still. *Knock. Knock. Knock.* "I'm

cold and hungry. Hungry and cold. Let me in. Let me innnnn..."

"Put a spell on the door," said the sixth witch.

"Lock it up tight," agreed the seventh.

Together the witches chanted, "Lock it. Lock it. Don't let anyone knock it."

Knock. Knock. Knock. "Look under the door. Look under the cupboard. Look under the petticoat's frilllll... Look under the covers. Look under the rafter. Look under the cauldron. Look under the window silllll... "

They looked and they saw. They looked again. Seven pans of biscuit dough. A pan for each. A biscuit feast. The dough began to rise. It rose high and higher still. It rose to the table. It rose to the window. It rose to the rafters. It rose to the loft. It crowded the floor. It crowded the furniture. It crowded the witches who ran to the door.

"It won't open!" cried the first.

"We're going to die!" moaned the second.

"Ladies, ladies, we must fly," said the third.

"We're not ready. The spell isn't done," said the fourth.

Knock. Knock. Knock. "Fly you must," came the windy voice. "Fly you will. Tonight and forever you'll fly and ask *whooooo...*"

The door opened with a creak and a crack. The wind blew in sounding like

Whooooo's that?

The witches turned into hoot owls and flapped their wings. They flew out the door and into the dark woods. They fly every Halloween night and ask, "Whooooo…whooooo…whooooo…"

Beware, beware on Halloween night. If you meet up with one of the seven, she'll turn you into a hoot-hoot-hoot owl, tooooo…

Whooooo… whooooo….

The Lost Fiddler

Wales

The Little Folk of Wales are known as the old and wise ones. Sometimes they are called elves. They live for ages and ages and can change themselves into animals and plants. They live everywhere and nowhere. The Little Folk are terribly shy. Seldom does a man or woman, boy or girl, actually see one.

Elves are full of mischief and enjoy playing tricks. They know that turnabout is fair play. If you play a trick on them, they'll laugh and be merry. But not on All Hallows

Eve. Be very careful on All Hallows Eve. The Little Folk won't tolerate a trick or a lie, or even a taste of foolishness on this night of all nights.

Long ago there was a fiddle player named Putnam. He lived by a large pond in the tree-thick forest. He practiced his fiddle day and night, night and day. His music floated throughout the woods. Birds sang, squirrels chattered, and mice squeaked, staying in tune. The Little Folk loved his music as well. They often came out of their hidden caves to leap up and down while dancing round and round.

One morning Putnam found a gold coin on his doorstep. He knew who had left it and wanted to have some fun. After milking his cow, he poured a cupful into an old tin can. The bottom of the can had a hole, which he stuffed with grass. When the chief of the Little Folk picked up the cup to carry it

home, all the milk ran out.

The chief returned the favor by placing another gold coin on Putnam's doorstep. When he tried to pick it up, it vanished into thin air. Both Putnam and the chief enjoyed a hearty laugh.

All Hallows Eve approached. The humans who lived in the village asked Putnam to play for the big celebration. He began practicing a new tune with his fiddle, day and night, night and day. The forest sang with the new symphony. The Little Folk heard it and liked what they heard. A gold coin wrapped in a green leaf lay on Putnam's doorstep the morning of the sacred eve. Human words were scratched on the leaf.

Play for us tonight.

"I will! I will!" shouted Putnam. "I'll come after I play for my people."

The human party began at dusk and lasted long into the night. People wore costumes that were funny and scary. They ate and drank and laughed and danced. Putnam played his fiddle for hours on end. The people loved his tunes and wouldn't let him rest. It grew late as the fiddler played on and on. The drink flowed freely, and the dancers didn't stop until dawn crept over the horizon.

Putnam ran out of the building, following

the road back into the forest. He'd promised
to play for the Little Folk on their special
night. He had not kept his promise.

He came to the mouth of a dark cave.
Odd, he thought, as he'd never before seen
the cave. A strange music was coming from
within. It sounded like a fiddle playing. It
sounded like his new tune. It sounded like
him.

Bending close to the ground, he entered
the cave. He crept forward on hands and
knees, being careful to not harm his fiddle.
He came to a great room and was amazed at
what he saw. Two hundred Little Folk,
dressed in clothes made of silver and gold,
danced to a fiddler who was as white as a
ghost. The fiddler looked like Putnam. The
fiddler played like Putnam. The fiddler was
Putnam.

He never returned to his home by the
pond. The humans who knew him wondered

where he had gone. They searched for days and shouted his name: "Putnam! Fiddler Putnam!"

You can still hear him play his special tune, but only on All Hallows Eve. Journey deep into the forest and wait until the moon rises high. Listen. You won't see the cave or the Little Folk, but you'll hear Putnam's fiddle on the night wind. It's his new song, the one he practiced over and over again. It's the ghost of Putnam fulfilling his promise made so long ago. And if you listen even more closely, you'll hear the sounds of two hundred Little Folk's tiny feet, dancing the night away.

Notes

The stories in this collection are my retellings of tales from throughout the world. They've come to me from both oral and written sources and result from thirty years of my telling them aloud.

Two of the tales (indicated by asterisks) were previously included in my two-volume set entitled *Pleasant Journeys: Tales to Tell from Around the World* (Mercer Island, Washington: The Writing Works, 1979) and later retitled *Twenty-Two Splendid Tales to Tell from Around the World* (Little Rock: August House Publishers, 1994).

Motifs given are from *the Storyteller's Sourcebook: A Subject, Title and Motif Index to Folklore Collections for Children* by Margaret Read MacDonald (Detroit: Neal-Schuman/Gale, 1982).

Twelve Months—Czechoslovakia

Motif Q2.1.4Ac. I love the fairy tale quality of this wonderful Cinderella variant and enjoy sharing it each New Year's Day. I was introduced to the story in *Favorite Fairy Tales Told in Czechoslovakia* by Virginia Haviland (Boston: Little, Brown, 1966), pp. 3-20. She discovered and retold it from *Fairy Tales of the Slav Peasants and Herdsmen,* from the French of Aleksandr

Borejko Chodzko; translated by Emily J. Harding (London: George Allen, 1896).

Another variant is found in *The Big Book of Stories From Many Lands* by Rhoda Power (New York: Watts, 1969), pp. 193-205.

Babushka — Russia

Motif N816.2. Wearing my bathrobe and a beard made of cardboard, I played one of the three wise men knocking on Babushka's door. It was in front of my elementary school classroom, long ago, during the Christmas season. I've remembered and told the haunting tale since. Create the longing of her search with the refrain, "Farther on, farther on..."

Two variants are found in *Baboushka and the Three Kings* by Ruth Robbins (Berkeley, California: Parnassus, 1960); and *The Youngest Storybook: A Collection of Stories and Rhymes for the Youngest* by Eileen Colwell (New York: Watts, 1967, 1968), pp. 249-252.

The Little Juggler — France

Motif V92. This beautiful French legend has been told for hundreds of years in a variety of ways. Perhaps the oldest known manuscript, written in Old French more than seven hundred years ago, is in Paris in the *Bibliotheque de l'Arsenal*. From the first time I heard it on a holiday radio program in 1966, I knew it was a story that I would tell. There simply is no better offering than the gift of ourselves.

Two beautifully written variants are found in *The Way of the Storyteller* by Ruth Sawyer (New York: Viking, 1962), pp. 273-281; and *The Little Juggler* by Barbara Cooney (New York: Hastings House, 1961).

Christina's Christmas Garden* — Scandinavia

Motif Q1.1. This story is pure delight to share. Describe the unexpected ending with an attitude of wonder and awe. It works. I first heard this story in 1975 at a Seattle country club's Christmas celebration. A Swedish grandmother sat me in a corner after my program and, in a hushed voice, began to tell. A dozen children and several parents had gathered round by the time she finished.

A variant is found in *Favorite Fairy Tales Told in Denmark* by Virginia Haviland (Boston: Little, Brown, 1971), pp. 77-90.

The Baker's Dozen* — United States

Motif V429.2 Living in the capital region of upstate New York, I see the colonial Dutch influence nearly everywhere I walk. Attitudes of caring and generosity are deeply imbedded in this ever-changing environment. The early tales speak true. I heard this story initially while living in New Salem, Massachusetts, in 1967. It was told to me by my neighbor, Harold Johnson.

For another version, see *With a Wig, With a Wag, and Other American Folk Tales* by Jean Cothran (New York: McKay, 1954), pp. 18-22.

The Hanukkah Bowl — Russia

Motif K112.2. The Jewish variant of the universally popular "Stone Soup," this has recently become one of my favorite holiday tales to share. Other variants include making latkes with a magic spoon and, in one case, beginning with just a crust of bread. But as happens in variants, the dish—be it soup, stew, or latkes—gets made through community contribution.

I first heard this variant while visiting a synagogue in Tucson, Arizona, in 1996. It was the week of Hanukkah, and the guest rabbi told it as part of the service.

See *The Hanukkah Anthology* by Philip Goodman (Philadelphia: The Jewish Publication Society of America, 1976), pp. 324-328. See also *The Jar of Fools: Eight Hanukkah Stories from Chelm* by Eric A. Kimmel (New York: Holiday House, 2000), pp. 27-34.

St. Valentine — Italy

I vividly recall making and decorating Valentine's

Day boxes each year in grade school in the late 1940s and early 1950s. I also recall signing cards for each member of the class and the party that followed. It was during these early years that I heard the legend of St. Valentine—and more than once, I'm certain, for it has always stayed with me. Because there were many Roman priests named Valentine during the time of this story, I doubt that the plot follows a true course. But the story is strong and remains in our universal consciousness. It's worth telling again.

A variant is found in *Holiday Roundup* by Frances Cavanah and Lucile Pannell (Philadelphia: Macrae Smith, 1950, 1968) pp. 40-41. See also *Hearts, Cupids, and Red Roses: The Story of the Valentine Symbols* by Edna Barth (New York: Seabury, 1974) pp. 8-30.

Whooooo—American South

Motif D153.2. This is my version of the famous Southern Halloween tale called "The Conjure Wives." It has developed over several years in front of thousands of primary students, in hundreds of elementary schools, throughout the United States. Naturally, you must have fun while telling and exaggerate the *whooooos*.

See *Ghosts and Goblins: Stories for Halloween* by Wilhelmina Harper (New York: Dutton, 1936), pp. 44-47; and *North American Legends* by Virginia Haviland (New York: Collins, 1979), pp. 122-125.

The Lost Fiddler—Wales

Motif E425.2.5.1. This tale, popular throughout the British Isles, echoes back to the days of yore when little folk, elves, and fairies were a natural part of the landscape—if not in reality, certainly in belief. I've long wanted to tell it with a fiddler at my side. This is a perfect tale to round out a Halloween program. Let's keep it alive, always.

Other variants are found in *The Talking Tree: Fairy Tales from Fifteen Lands* by Augusta Baker (Philadelphia: Lippincott, 1955), pp. 45-47; and *Scottish Folk-Tales and Legends* by Barbara Ker Wilson (New York: Oxford University Press, 1954), pp. 28-32.